DIE KLARINETTE

Die Klarinette lässt sich in *fünf Einzelteile* inklusive des Mundstücks zerlegen und ist so leichter zu transportieren. Wie andere Holzblasinstrumente auch, hat die Klarinette ein ausgeklügeltes System aus Klappen und Hebeln, um die einzelnen Löcher zu schließen oder zu öffnen. Es gibt verschiedene Griffsysteme für Klarinette: Das *Boehm-System* und das *Oehler-System*.

Die Klarinette ist ein Instrument mit *einfachem Rohrblatt*. Das flache Rohrblatt wird von außen am Mundstück befestigt. Der Ton entsteht, wenn der Spieler durch das schmale Loch im Mundstück bläst und somit das Blatt zum Vibrieren bringt.

DIE PFLEGE DER KLARINETTE

1. Nach dem Spielen nimmst du das Blatt ab und legst es in einen Blatthalter. Dort kann es richtig trocknen, und es hält länger.
2. Reinige jedes Stück von innen mit einem Wischer. Damit der Wischer nicht stecken bleibt, solltest du ihn immer in der Richtung des Luftstroms von oben nach unten durchziehen.
3. Damit die Klappen immer glänzen, solltest du sie mit einem weichen Tuch abreiben.
4. Bewahre nur Dinge in deinem Klarinettenkoffer auf, die hineinpassen. Wenn du Noten und andere Dinge hineinquetschst, kann das Instrument beschädigt werden.

MOUTF
MUNI

BARREL
BIRNE

:R
(Blattschraube)

UPPER SECTION
OBERSTÜCK

TONE HOLE RINGS
KLAPPEN

LOWER SECTION
UNTERSTÜCK

TONE HOLE RINGS
KLAPPEN

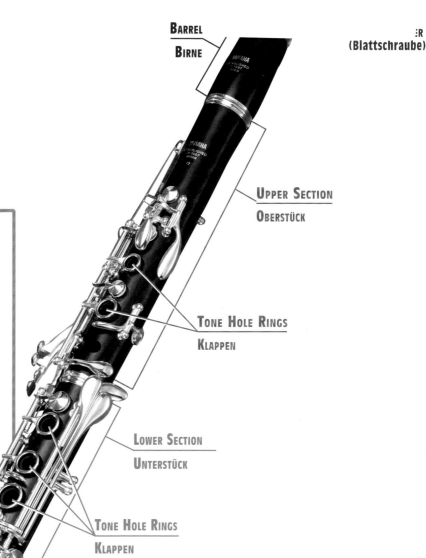

BELL
SCHALLSTÜCK

THE CLARINET

The clarinet divides into *five sections* including the mouthpiece. This design makes it easier to carry around. Like other woodwind instruments, clarinets have a complicated system of keys and levers to open and close the holes in the pipe.

There are different key systems for clarinet, i.e. the *Boehm-system* and the *Oehler-system*.

The clarinet is a *single-reed* instrument. The flat cane reed is fixed to the outside of the mouthpiece, and when the player blows through the narrow hole in the mouthpiece, the reed vibrates to produce the sound.

CLARINET CARE

1. When you are finished playing, take off the reed and place it in a reed holder. This allows the reed to dry properly and makes it last longer.
2. Use the clarinet swab to dry the inside of each section. To avoid getting the swab stuck, always pull it through in the same direction as the flow of air, from top to bottom.
3. To keep your keys shiny, wipe them off with a soft cloth.
4. Store only those items in your case that the case is designed to hold. Forcing sheet music or other objects into your clarinet case can cause problems with the instrument.

Der Tonumfang | Tone Range

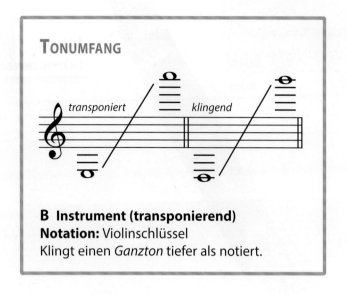

B Instrument (transponierend)
Notation: Violinschlüssel
Klingt einen *Ganzton* tiefer als notiert.

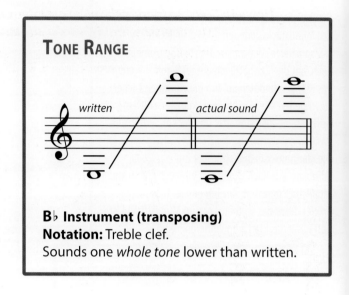

B♭ Instrument (transposing)
Notation: Treble clef.
Sounds one *whole tone* lower than written.

Die Griffweise

The Fingerings

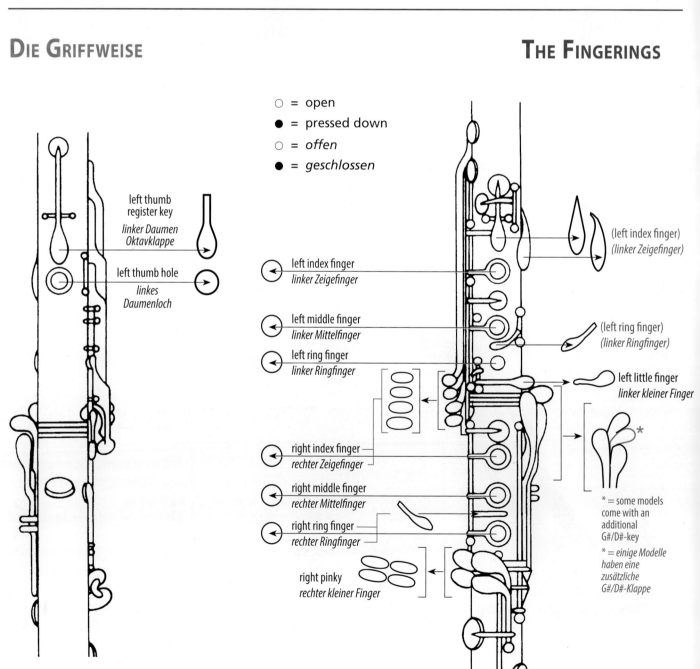

○ = open
● = pressed down
○ = *offen*
● = *geschlossen*

left thumb register key
linker Daumen Oktavklappe

left thumb hole
linkes Daumenloch

(left index finger)
(linker Zeigefinger)

left index finger
linker Zeigefinger

left middle finger
linker Mittelfinger

left ring finger
linker Ringfinger

(left ring finger)
(linker Ringfinger)

left little finger
linker kleiner Finger

right index finger
rechter Zeigefinger

right middle finger
rechter Mittelfinger

right ring finger
rechter Ringfinger

right pinky
rechter kleiner Finger

* = some models come with an additional G#/D#-key

* = *einige Modelle haben eine zusätzliche G#/D#-Klappe*

KLARINETTEN-GRIFFTABELLE *Boehm System* CLARINET FINGERING CHART

Hinweis: *Diese Ausgabe gebraucht die international übliche Stammtonbezeichnung C D E F G A B.*
Der deutsche Ton „H" wird also als „B" bezeichnet, das deutsche „B" als „B♭".

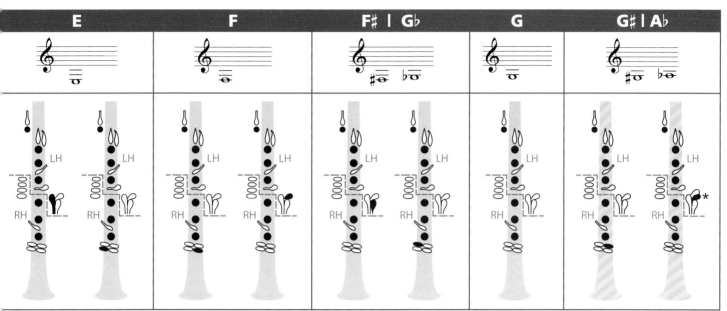

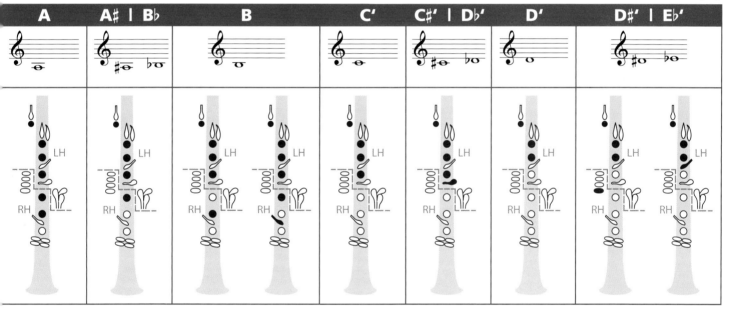

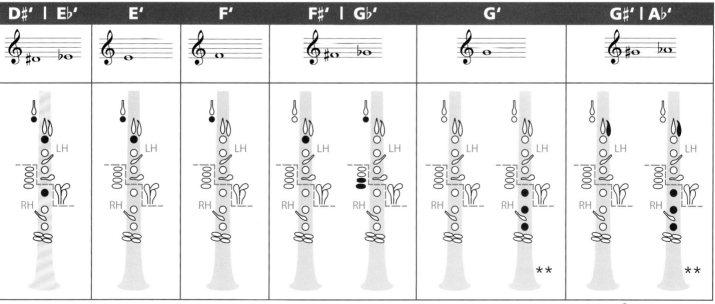

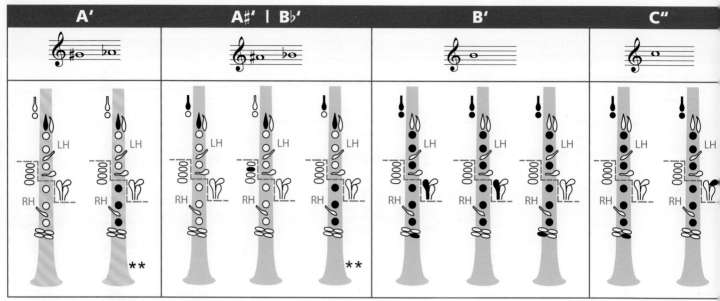

** = Alternativgriff für den einfacheren Übergang ins mittlere Register
** = alternate fingering to facilitate register change to middle register

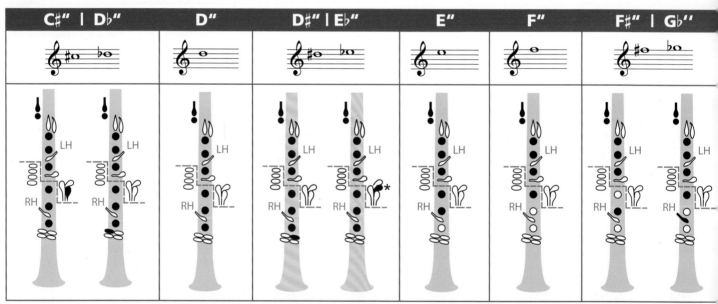

* = for instruments with G#-key only
* = nur für Instrumente mit G#-Klappe

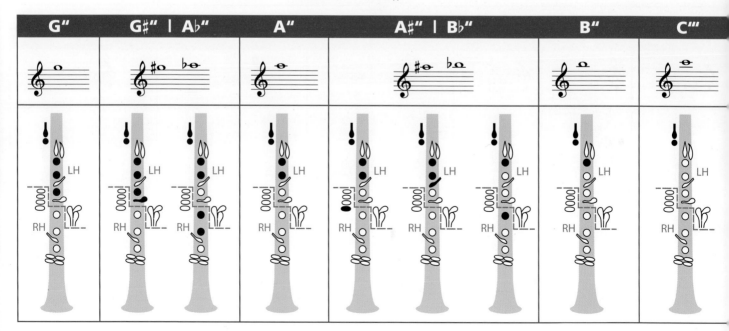

Boehm System

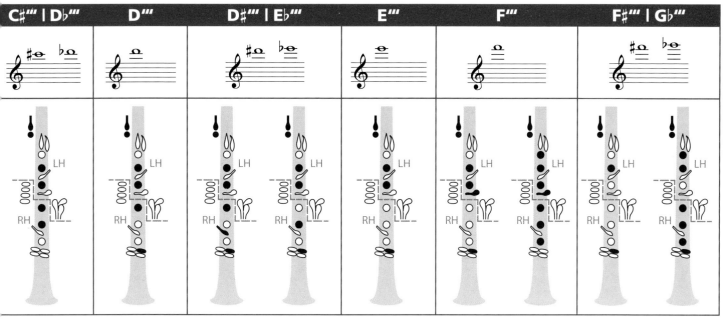

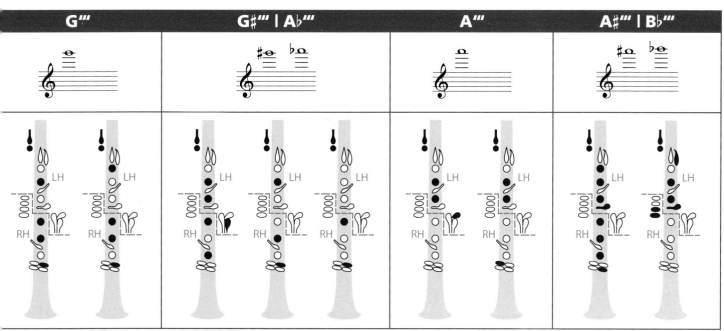

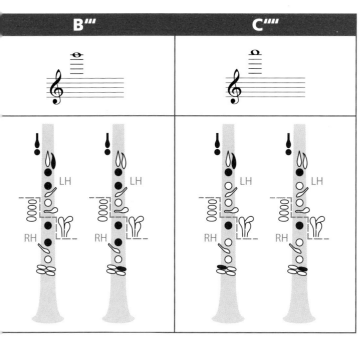

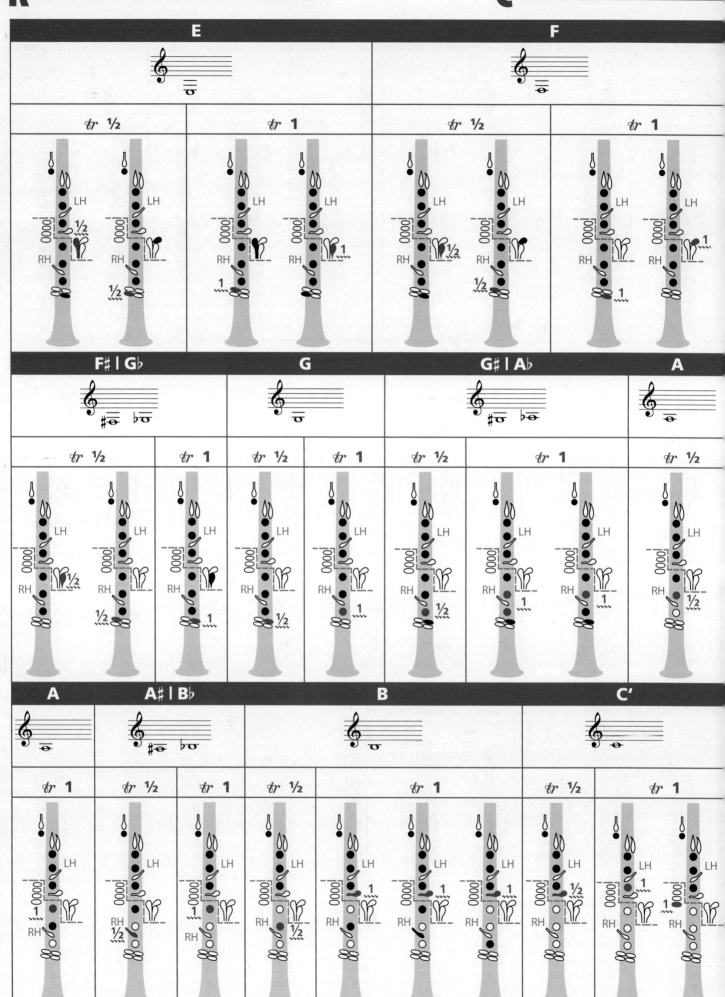

Boehm System

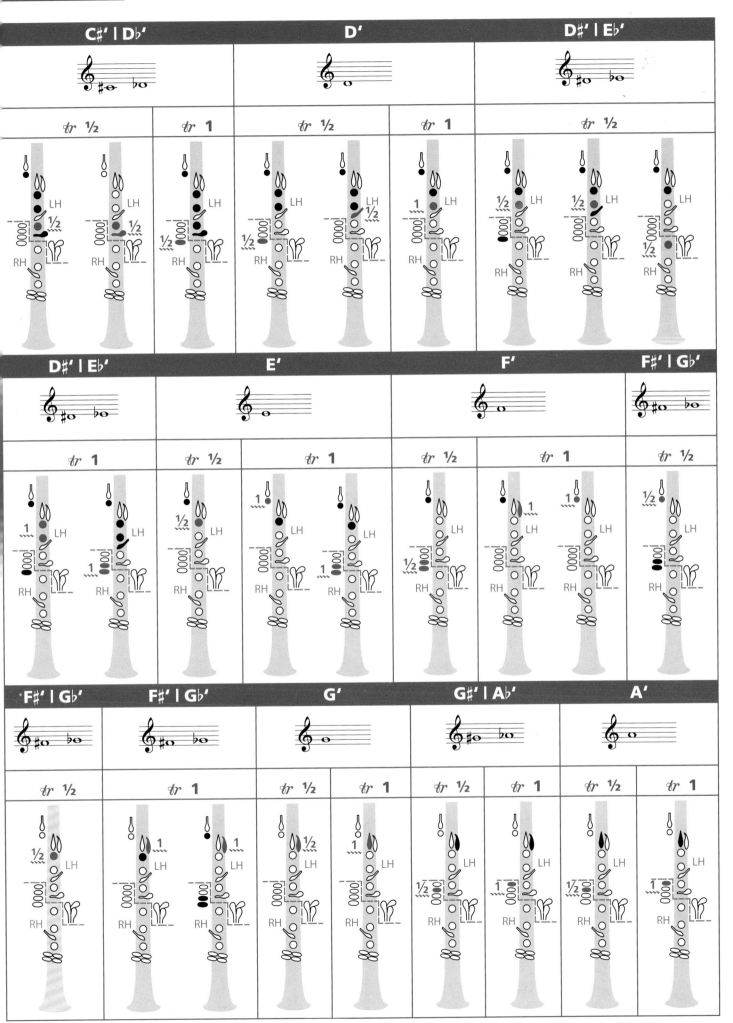

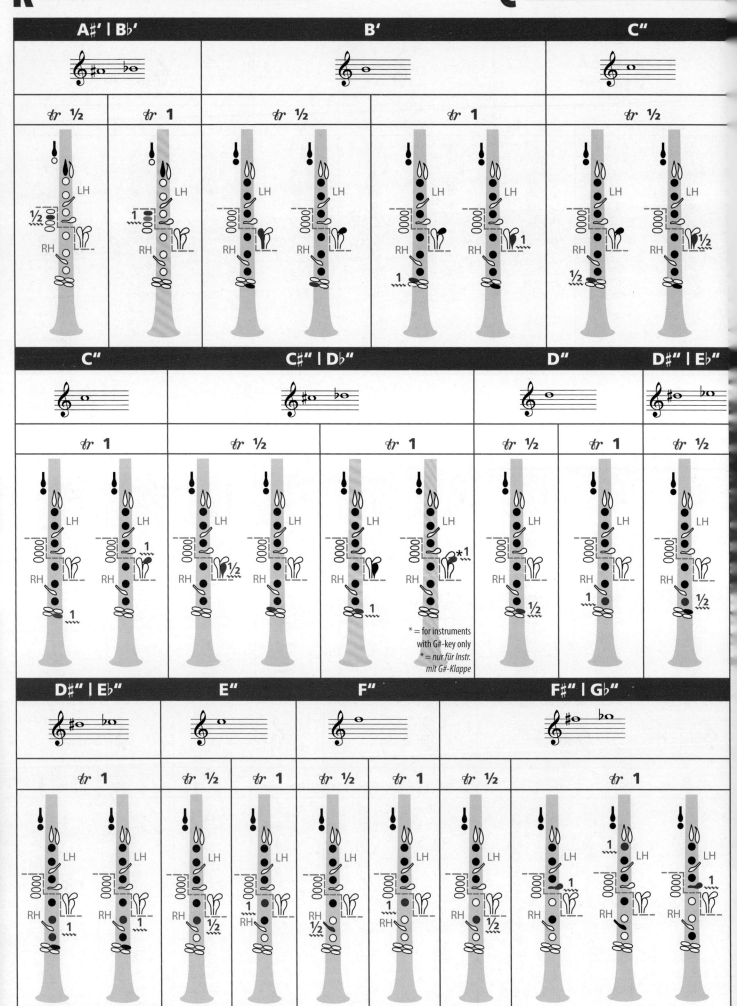

* = for instruments
with G#-key only
* = nur für Instr.
mit G#-Klappe

Boehm System

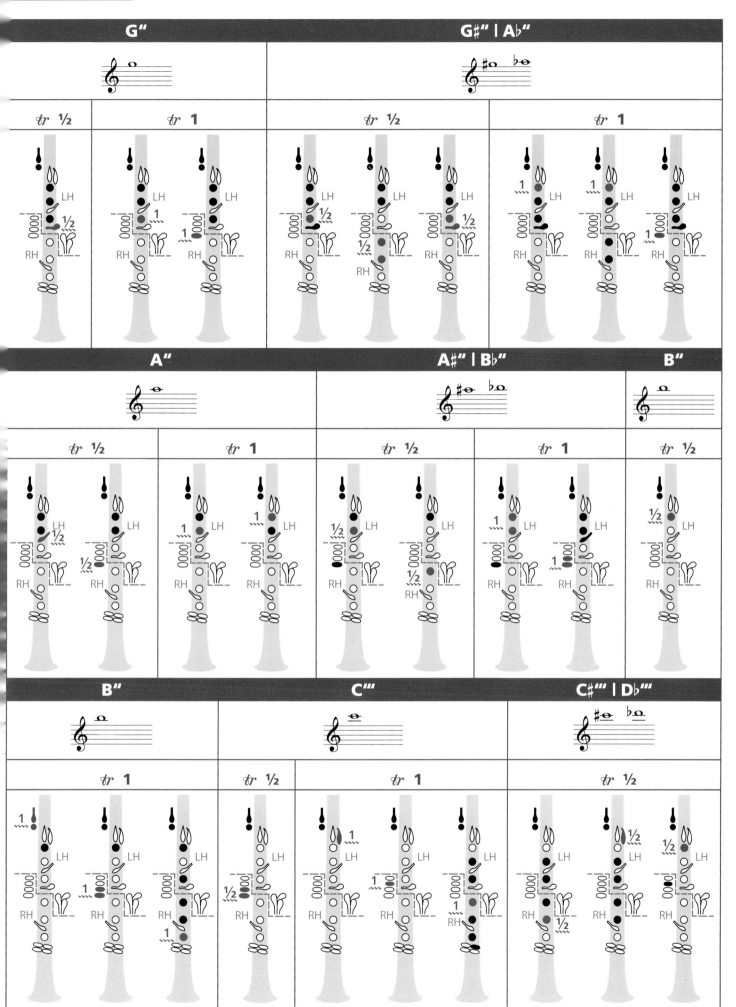

KLARINETTEN-TRILLERTABELLE

CLARINET TRILL CHART

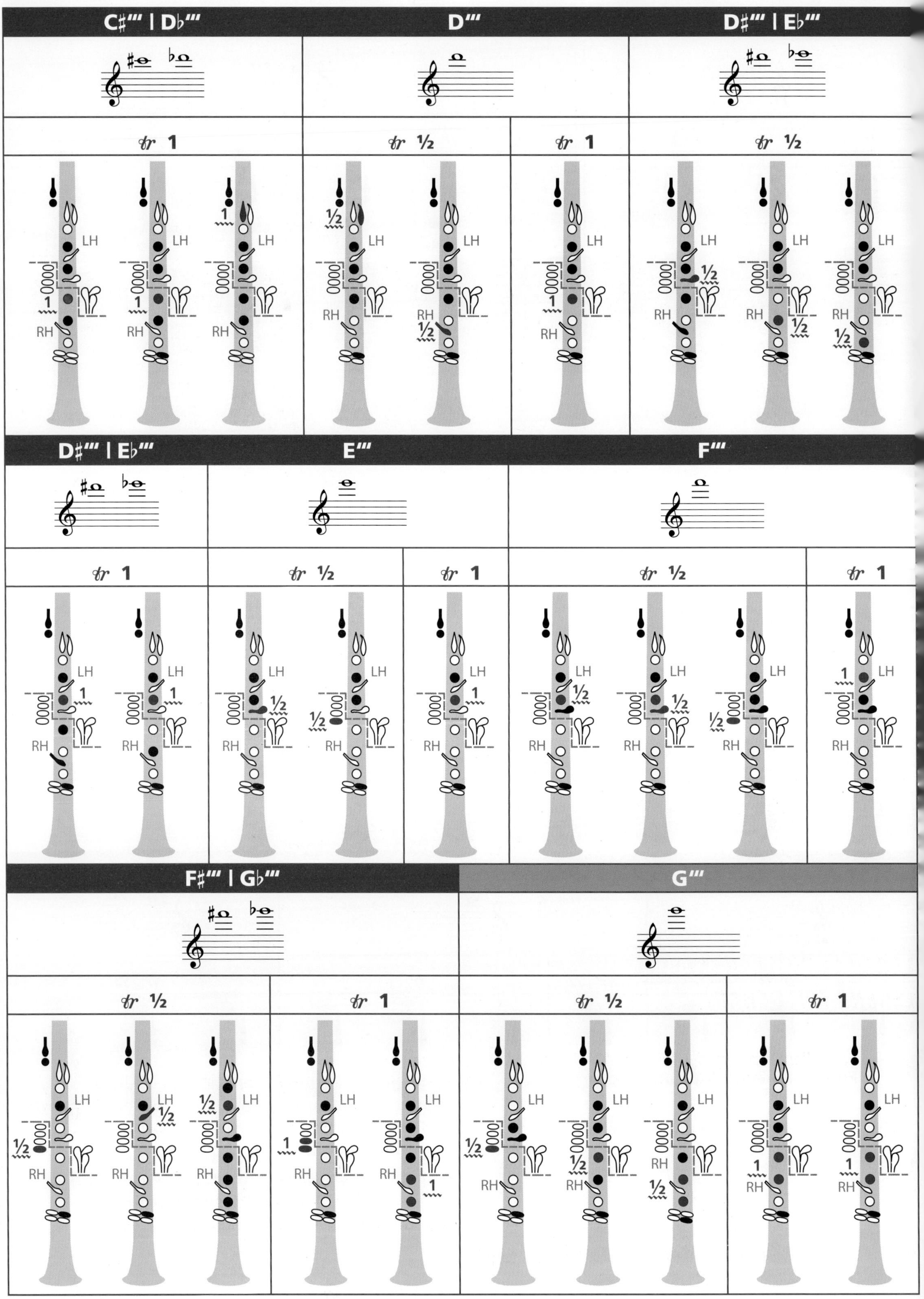

Boehm System

	G#'''' | Ab''''			A''''			A#'''' | Bb''''	
	tr ½	*tr* 1		*tr* ½	*tr* 1		*tr* ½	*tr* 1	

	B''''			C''''	
	tr ½	*tr* 1		*tr* ½	*tr* 1

LEGENDE TRILLERTABELLE
LEGEND TRILL CHART

⬤ = *Schnelles Öffnen und Schließen der Klappen*
    = Rapid alternation (open/close key)

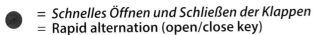

1 ⬤ = *tr* **1** = *Ganzton-Triller* | Wholetone trill

½ ⬤ = *tr* **½** = *Halbton-Triller* | Halftone trill

Please note:
The trills in the high range from G''' and up (here highlighted in green) are quite difficult to play. The shown fingerings can vary on each individual instrument.

Hinweis:
Die (grün hervorgehobenen) Triller ab G''' aufwärts sind schon sehr schwer zu spielen. Die angegebenen Griffe können von Instrument zu Instrument variieren.

⬤ = *Griffloch optional schließen* | close hole optionally

FORMING THE EMBOUCHURE

Embouchure is a French word used to describe the way you shape your mouth while playing. Here is how to form a good embouchure:

1. Turn your lower lip slightly over your bottom teeth to provide a cushion for the reed.
2. Place the reed on your lower lip so that it extends about 1/2 inch into your mouth.
3. Place your upper teeth on top of the mouthpiece.
4. Tighten the corners of your mouth while saying "oo." Stretch your chin so that it remains pointed and flat.

PRODUCING YOUR FIRST TONE

1. Practice taking a full breath, filling the bottom of your lungs so that your stomach expands. Then fill the top of your lungs without raising your shoulders. With gentle pressure, exhale completely. Always using a full breath while playing helps to produce long, full tones.
2. Our first tone will be produced using just the mouthpiece and barrel. Hold the assembled mouthpiece and barrel sections, form an embouchure and take a full breath through the corners of your mouth. Lift your tongue slightly so that it contacts the reed. Now start to exhale and then release the reed as if saying "*Too.*" Make the tone last as long as possible.

   Next, produce several notes on one breath by touching the reed with your tongue as if saying "*Too-Too-Too-Too—*" while exhaling. Produce as many notes as possible on one breath until you run out of air.

PRACTICE TIPS

1. Try to find a place with a good, firm chair where you will not be interrupted. Use a music stand to hold your music in the correct position for playing.
2. Occasionally use different reeds so that you will always have more than one reed ready for performance.
3. Start by playing long tones. This builds your embouchure and improves your tone.
4. Always include some already learned "review" pieces, so that you continue to improve and perfect your performance.
5. Spend a concentrated period of time on the most difficult parts of your music. Avoid the temptation to play only the easy parts.
6. To make your practice even more enjoyable, try playing along with play-along CDs.

DER ANSATZ

Der Begriff *Ansatz* bezeichnet die Mundhaltung beim Spielen. Und so sieht ein guter Ansatz aus:

1. Wölbe die Unterlippe leicht über die unteren Schneidezähne, um ein elastisches Polster für das Blatt zu bilden.
2. Setze das Blatt auf der Unterlippe auf, so dass es ca. 1,5 cm weit in den Mundraum ragt.
3. Lege die oberen Schneidezähne auf das Mundstück auf.
4. Spanne die Mundwinkel an und sage dabei *„oh"*. Strecke das Kinn so, dass es spitz und flach bleibt.

DEIN ERSTER TON

1. Atme tief ein, so dass sich der untere Teil der Lunge mit Luft füllt und sich der Bauch vorwölbt. Fülle anschließend den oberen Teil der Lunge mit Luft, ohne die Schultern anzuheben. Atme dann mit leichtem Druck vollständig aus. Langes, tiefes Ein- und Ausatmen beim Spielen trägt zur Erzeugung langer, voller Töne bei.
2. Unser erster Ton wird mit Hilfe des Mundstücks und der Birne erzeugt. Halte das an der Birne befestigte Mundstück, forme einen Ansatz und hole durch die Mundwinkel tief Luft. Hebe die Zunge leicht an, so dass sie Kontakt mit dem Blatt bekommt. Jetzt beginnst du auszuatmen und lässt das Blatt los, als ob du *„tu"* sagen würdest. Halte den Ton so lange wie möglich aus. Als nächstes spielst du mehrere Töne in einem Atemzug, indem du das Blatt mit der Zunge berührst, als wolltest du *„tu-tu-tu—"* sagen, während du ausatmest. Erzeuge in einem Atemzug so viele Töne wie möglich, bis dir die Luft ausgeht.

ÜBUNGSTIPPS

1. Suche dir einen ungestörten Platz mit einem guten, stabilen Stuhl. Benutze für deine Noten einen Notenständer in der richtigen Spielhöhe.
2. Benutze gelegentlich verschiedene Blätter, damit du immer mehr als ein Blatt zum Spielen zur Verfügung hast.
3. Beginne mit dem Spielen langer Töne. Das trägt zur Verbesserung deines Ansatzes und der Tonqualität bei.
4. Spiele immer auch ein paar „Wiederholungsstücke", die du schon gelernt hast, damit du dich weiter verbesserst und dein Spiel perfektionierst.
5. Konzentriere dich einige Zeit auf die schwierigsten Stellen deiner Stücke. Du solltest der Versuchung widerstehen, nur die leichten Stellen zu spielen.
6. Um mehr Spaß am Üben zu bekommen, kannst du mit Play-along CDs spielen.

Klezmer Play-alongs für Klarinette | for Clarinet
20139G (deutsch) | ISBN 978-3-9331-3664-0
20139US (english) | ISBN 978-3-9331-3690-9

Balkan-Duette für Klarinette | for Clarinet
20140G (deutsch) | ISBN 978-3-933136-65-7
20140US (english) | ISBN 978-3-9331-3691-6

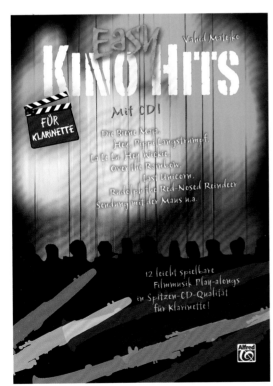

Easy Kino Hits für Klarinette
20177G (deutsch) | ISBN 978-3-943638-10-3
Kino Hits für Klarinette
20178G (deutsch) | ISBN 978-3-943638-11-0

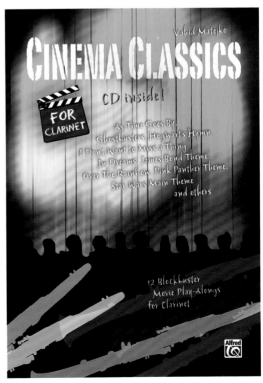

Cinema Classics for Clarinet
20222G (english) | ISBN 978-3-943638-56-1

for Clarinet Oehler System
20228G | ISBN 978-3-943638-62-2

for Soprano | Alto | Tenor | Baritone Saxophone
20229G | ISBN 978-3-943638-63-9

for Flute
20226G | ISBN 978-3-943638-60-8

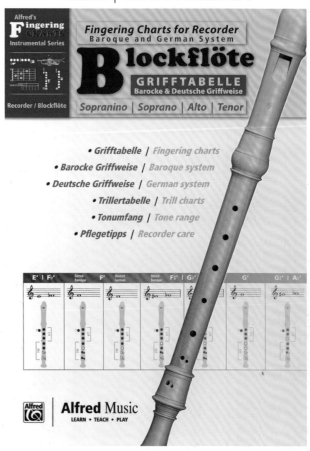

for Sopranino | Soprano | Alto | Tenor Recorder
20232G | ISBN 978-3-943638-66-0

© 2013 by **Alfred** Music Publishing GmbH
info@alfredverlag.de
alfredmusic.de | alfredverlag.de
Redaktionelle Mitarbeit: K. Dapper und W. Güdden
Including excerpts from Accent on Achievement (00-17084G)
All Rights Reserved! | Printed in Germany

9 783943 638615